for Luna

To my wife Ellegra, I know you know I couldn't have done this without you.

One day, Luna took a poo.

She flushed the toilet, but the poo did not go away. Luna did not know what to do.

But, you must leave," Luna said as she washed her hands, "I have to get ready for the day.

"I can help you", said the poo. "I'll help you get ready for the day, before I go away."

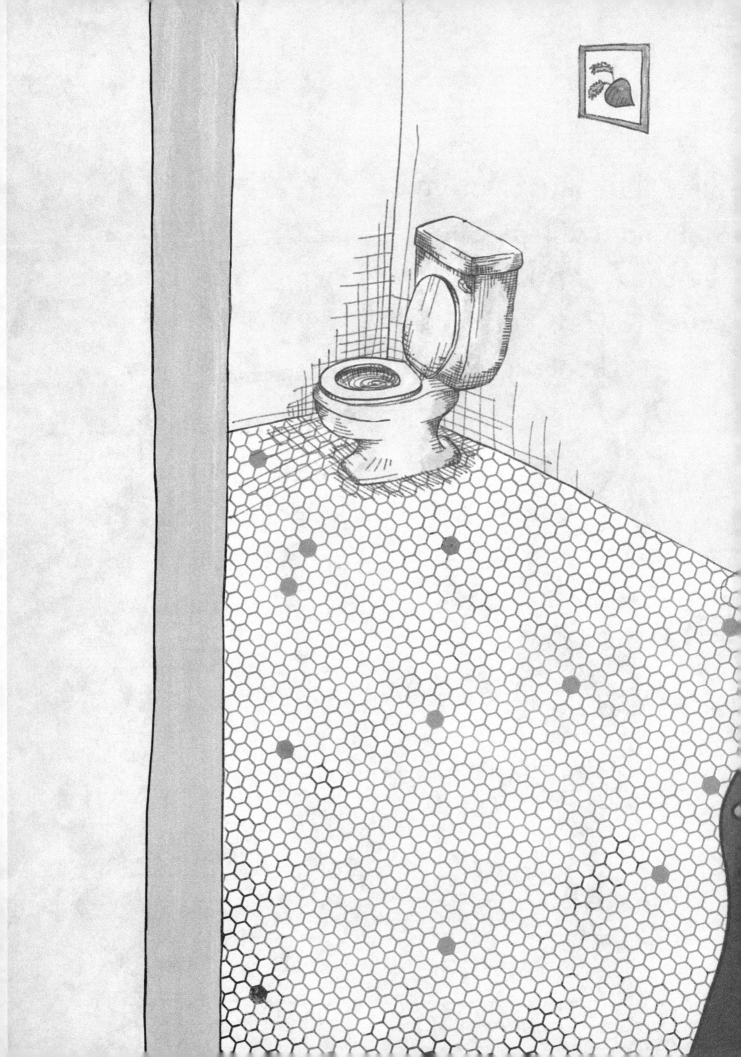

"I do not need your help, poo. I'm asking you politely, please go away." Luna said as she brushed her teeth.

But the poo ignored her and continued it's plea.

"Of course you need me. You'll do everything wrong, as far as I can see."

Luna continued with her routine and tried to ignore the pesky poo.

Next she brushed her hair, it was her favorite thing to do.

Luna brushed out her hair till it was silky and smooth.

She swooped
and
looped...

Luna threw
her feet into
her favorite
pair of shoes.

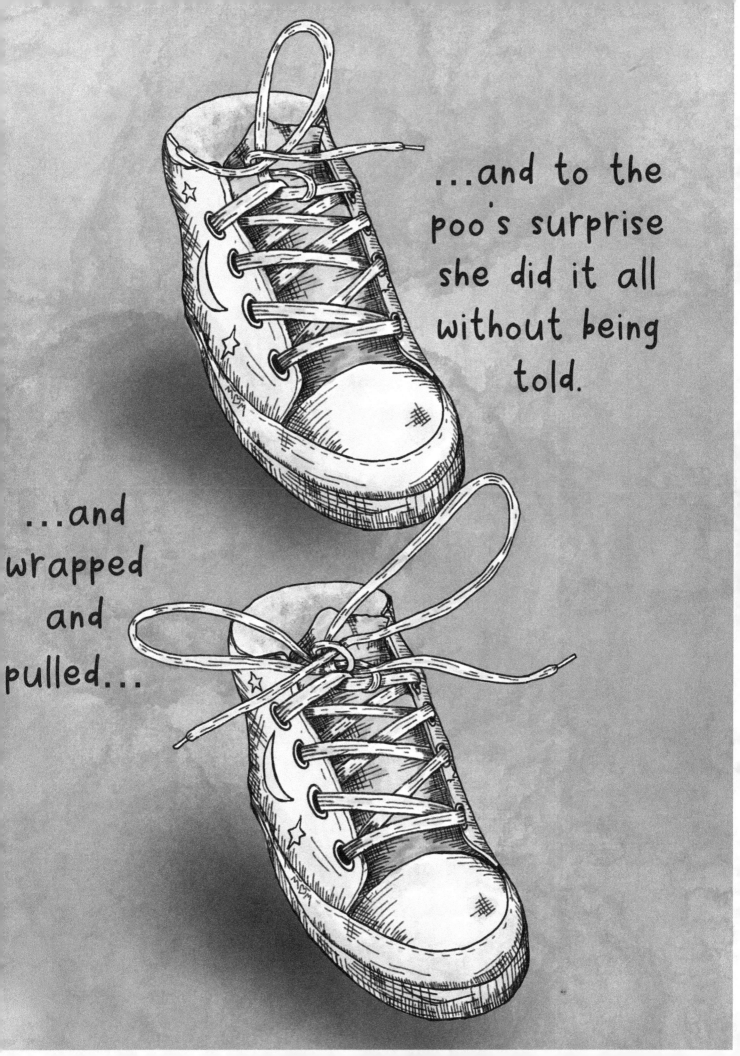

...and to the poo's surprise she did it all without being told.

...and wrapped and pulled...

And with that, Luna flushed again and the poo went away.

Luna ran out the door...

CPSIA information can be obtained
at www.ICGtesting.com
Printed in the USA
BVHW021947160223
658636BV00030B/86